POPPY'S BABIES

For Lizzie and Peter

First American edition published in 1995 by Philomel Books,
a division of The Putnam & Grosset Group,
200 Madison Avenue, New York, NY 10016.
Philomel Books, Reg. U.S. Pat. & Tm. Off.
Originally published in 1994 by HarperCollins Publishers, Ltd., London.
Printed and bound in Italy.

Library of Congress Cataloging-in-Publication Data
Barklem, Jill. Poppy's babies/by Jill Barklem.
p.cm.(Brambly Hedge)
Summary: Dusty surprises Poppy with a new house on the day
their babies receive names from Old Vole.
ISBN 0-399-22743-1
[1. Mice-Fiction. 2. Babies-Fiction. 3. Dwellings-Fiction.]
I. Title.   II. Series: Barklem, Jill. Brambly Hedge.
P27.B25058Po 1995 [E]- -dc20 93-50807 CIP AC
1 3 5 7 9 10 8 6 4 2
First American Edition

POPPY'S BABIES

Jill Barklem

PHILOMEL BOOKS
NEW YORK

It was the beginning of summer. Outside, the trees were in leaf and sunshine sparkled on the stream. The mill wheel turned in the cool shadows of the riverbank, and inside the mill Dusty Dogwood was busy grinding the corn for the mice of Brambly Hedge.

Poppy was upstairs trying to persuade her new babies to go to sleep but every time they closed their eyes, the clatter of the mill shook the floorboards and woke them up again.

She opened the door to the stairs and a cloud of flour dust blew into her face.

"Dusty, please finish soon. It's time for the babies' nap."

"I'll do my best," he called back.

The babies were still awake when two visitors peeped round the door.

"Do you know that there are ninety-two stairs up to your kitchen?" gasped Primrose.

"However do you manage with the babies?" asked Lady Woodmouse, giving Poppy a kiss.

"It's very difficult," Poppy replied. She looked as though she were about to cry.

"How sweet they are," said Lady Woodmouse. "This one looks just like Dusty."

"That's Rose. Here is Buttercup, and the little one is Pipkin."

"I can't wait for their Naming Day," said Primrose. "When is it?"

"Just two days away!" said Lady Woodmouse.

At last the mill wheels stopped turning and the babies slept. The visitors tiptoed out and Poppy sat down to rest. She was exhausted.

Dusty bagged up the flour and went over to the Store Stump. He found Mr. Apple sitting at his workshop door, putting the finishing touches to a wooden mouse on wheels.

Wilfred, who was meant to be helping, was finding it much more amusing to play in the wood shavings.

"Hello, Dusty," said Mr. Apple. "How are those babies of yours?"

"Noisy," laughed Dusty, "but great fun. Poppy is not so happy though. The mill is a very inconvenient place to live. It's noisy, dusty and damp, and has far too many stairs."

"Come and live at our house," offered Wilfred.
"My mother loves babies."

"Thank you, Wilfred, but I fancy your mother
has enough on her hands with the four of you."

"I wonder what we can do to help Poppy,"
said Mr. Apple sympathetically.

Dusty returned later in the day to collect some wood for a repair to the mill.

"Come with me," said Mr. Apple. Dusty and Wilfred followed him to a little cottage in a hawthorn tree next to the Store Stump.

"I've never noticed this house before," said Dusty.

"It's been empty for years. I use it to keep my timber dry," said Mr. Apple.

While Dusty chose a suitable plank, Wilfred peered at an old cooking range.

"Does this still work?" he asked.

"I expect so," said Mr. Apple. "It used to be very cozy when my aunt lived here." Suddenly he raised a paw. "Dusty, Wilfred has given me an idea. Suppose we clean the cottage and paint it. Would it suit you and Poppy?"

Dusty thought for a moment and then he said excitedly, "You know, I think it might!"

"Poppy would love this," Dusty said, looking at a small sunny room. "It's just the right size for a nursery."

"Let's get everything ready for Naming Day," said Mr. Apple. "Do you think we can keep it a secret?" He looked pointedly at Wilfred.

"I won't say anything," said Wilfred. "Promise."

Mr. Apple and Wilfred went off to Crabapple
Cottage to tell Mrs. Apple about the plan
and Dusty hurried home to help give
the babies their bath.

"Look," cried Poppy.
"Buttercup's learnt to crawl."

Dusty lifted her up and gave her a hug.

"I do wish we lived somewhere else," said
Poppy. "I have to watch them every minute of
the day."

Mrs. Apple had alerted all the mice along the hedge and early next morning they began to arrive at Mayblossom Cottage with buckets and brooms. The windows were opened wide and the floors swept, sanded and scrubbed. Mrs. Apple wiped down the dresser shelves and cleaned out the cupboards and Mrs. Toadflax polished the bath. Dusty lit a pile of twigs in each grate to check that the chimneys weren't blocked.

"Now for the whitewash," said Mr. Apple. "Do you want to mix it, Wilfred?"

"As soon as the walls are dry, we can start to fetch the furniture from the mill," said Dusty.

"But how can we do that without Poppy seeing?"

"Ah, Mrs. Apple's thought of a plan," said Mr. Apple.

The next day Lady Woodmouse and Poppy sat
under the hedge, sewing. Bees buzzed in and out of
the flowers in the early morning sunshine and the
scent of hawthorn blossom filled the air.

"There, that quilt's finished," said Lady Woodmouse, putting the last stitch into a yellow flower.

"I've still got Pipkin's gown to make," sighed Poppy. "However am I going to finish it in time?"

"We've had a good idea," said Lady Woodmouse. "Why don't you all come and stay at the Palace with us tonight. We can work on the gowns together and Primrose can help you to dress the babies for Naming Day tomorrow morning."

"That would help Dusty too," said Poppy. "He seems to be very busy at the moment."

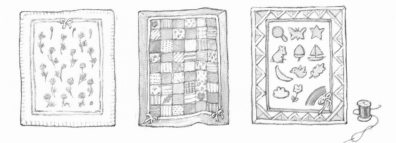

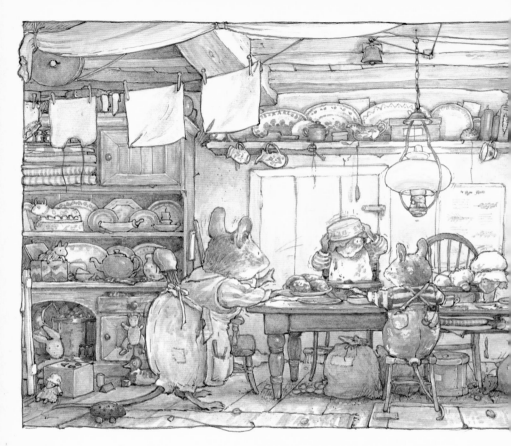

By late that afternoon, the cottage was almost ready. Wilfred put a last coat of whitewash on the nursery walls and Dusty measured up for the furniture.

"There, everything fits," he said with satisfaction. "Let's go back to the mill for tea."

"Goodness, whatever have you two been
doing?" asked Poppy, staring at Wilfred's fur.

"Painting," said Wilfred proudly. "I mean . . ."

"Something for the babies," said Dusty
quickly.

"You are a kind mouse, Wilfred," said Poppy.

Up and down Brambly Hedge, the mice were all busy. In the Palace kitchen, Mrs. Crustybread was making a special cake and her daughter Cicely made rosepetal butter and creamy junket.

Over at Mayblossom Cottage, Mrs. Toadflax had laid the table and was now hanging curtains, while up in the nursery, Lady Woodmouse unpacked the three little quilts.

"We're ready to fetch Poppy now," she said.

"Right," said Dusty. "As soon as you're at the Palace, we'll start to move in the furniture."

Down at the mill, Poppy was busy packing.

"There seems to be so much to take," she said, folding up three little nightgowns. "Perhaps I should stay here after all."

"No, no," said Lady Woodmouse hastily. "Primrose will be so disappointed if you don't come."

Eventually, they managed to get the nappies, bottles, toys, prams and babies down the stairs (all ninety-two of them!) and were ready to set off to the Palace.

The babies loved the journey. Rose gurgled
when she saw the stream, Pipkin threw his rattle
in the water, and when they reached the field,
Buttercup tried to get out of the pram.

At the door of Old Oak Palace, Dusty kissed
his family goodnight.

"Don't wait up for me," he said, "I've one or
two things to sort out before tomorrow."

The babies were bathed and put into their nightgowns. They were so excited by their new surroundings that they didn't want to settle, but at last they all fell asleep in the quiet of the hedgerow evening.

Lady Woodmouse lit the lamp, then she and Poppy sat and stitched the last of the lace onto the babies' gowns.

"How peaceful it is here," said Poppy.

As she spoke, a curious squeaking, bumping noise came through the open window.

"Whatever is that?" Poppy asked, startled.

Lady Woodmouse got up quickly and drew the curtains.

"Just Lord Woodmouse tidying up," she said. "We'd better get to bed. We'll need to be up before first light tomorrow."

Very early next morning, all the mice
gathered beneath the hawthorns for the
Naming Ceremony.

As dawn broke, Poppy handed Old Vole
the first baby. He cradled the little mouse in
his paws.

"The buds on the branches blossom and flower,
The blackbirds sing in the leafy bower,
And over the hill comes the rising sun,
To shine on the fields, and on you, little one."

"We name you Rose," said Old Vole, gently.

Just as Old Vole named the last baby Pipkin, the mice heard the patter of raindrops on the leaves.

"Oh dear, we'll all get wet," cried Poppy.

"No, no. Come this way," said Lady Woodmouse. "Bring the babies."

Poppy and Dusty ran toward the Store Stump and Dusty stood aside to let Poppy take shelter in the open door of a cottage.

Poppy found herself in the kitchen. Bright china that looked rather familiar was arranged on the dresser shelves and garlands of flowers hung from newly washed beams.

"What a dear little house," said Poppy.

"Let's look around," said Dusty.

Leaving Primrose in charge of the babies, Poppy and Dusty climbed the stairs.

"It's so cozy," she said as they reached the landing. "I wonder who lives here?"

Dusty led her to a small room that was warm and bright. Fresh curtains hung at the windows and beneath them stood three little cots, each with its own embroidered quilt. One was pink, one was yellow and one was blue.

"But Dusty . . ." Poppy cried.

"Yes," said Dusty, "With love from all your friends in Brambly Hedge. Welcome home!"

Poppy threw her paws round Dusty.

"This is the nicest surprise I've ever had," she said, then she ran downstairs to thank each mouse in turn.

"It's time to cut the cake!" shouted Wilfred.

Everyone was given a large slice and Basil served a summer punch with flowers floating on top. There were cowslip and violet salads, rosepetal sandwiches, primrose pottage and meadowsweet tea.

The babies crawled around underfoot and Poppy was glad of Mr. Apple's gates on the stairs. Then they were given some cake and got very sticky. Soon Rose began to cry, followed by Buttercup, and Pipkin rolled under the table.

"Poor babies, you're tired," said Poppy. "I'm going to tuck you into your cots."

The baby mice snuggled under their new quilts and by the time Poppy bent to kiss them, they were fast asleep. She tiptoed back downstairs to join the guests in the kitchen.

Mr. Apple proposed a toast.

"To the babies," he whispered, "and their new home."

"To Rose, Buttercup and Pipkin," added Mrs. Apple. "Bless their little whiskers."